Jane Eyre

Charlotte Brontë

Sweet
Cherry

Mrs Reed m. John Reed

Mrs Eyre m. Mr Eyre

John Reed

Eliza Reed

Georgina Reed

Jane Eyre

John Eyre

Miss Eyre m. Mr Rivers

St John Rivers   Mary Rivers

Diana Rivers

Chapter One

'Go and sit somewhere else until you can be a good, sweet little girl!'

I looked at my aunt's scowling face.

'But what have I done?' I asked. I couldn't think of anything I had done to upset her.

'Don't answer back!' she said.

My three cousins glared at me and huddled closer to their mother around the fire. I went into the breakfast room, climbed onto the window seat and pulled the curtain across. At least I was on my own here. I huddled against the rain-splattered window and looked out onto the grey, bleak moors. The wind howled and I shivered.

I opened the book about birds I had taken from the bookshelf.

Suddenly, the curtains were pulled open. My cousin, John, stood there. He had a nasty grin on his face. He snatched the book from my hands.

'Leave our things alone!' he shouted. 'Mother looks after you out of kindness, and this is how you behave. Go and stand by the door!'

I did so. John was a big boy of fourteen – four years older than me.

I waited. I knew something must be coming. Then, John

flung the book at me, and it hit my head.

It was so unfair. I felt a burning anger bubble up inside me. I screamed, 'Wicked boy!'

He lunged at me and grabbed my hair.

The pain brought tears to my eyes. I pushed him away and he fell to the floor.

'Rat! Rat!' he shouted.

Suddenly my aunt, Mrs Reed, was standing over me.

'Bessie!' she called to the maid.
'Take her away and lock her in the
Red Room.'

Bessie and another servant
grabbed my arms and dragged me
into the Red Room. They sat me on
a chair and said
they would tie me

to it if I didn't stop struggling.

'Shame on you for hitting your master,' said Bessie, but she had a kind voice and I knew she wasn't very angry at me.

'He is not my master! I am not a servant.'

'No, you are less than a servant,' said the other maid. 'You do nothing to pay for your keep.'

It was true. My aunt resented having to look after me. That was my only wrongdoing, and there was nothing I could do about it.

Bessie and the maid left me alone in the dark room. I heard a key turn in the lock.

Chapter Two

The Red Room was the best bedroom in the house. It had a grand four-poster bed, red carpet and red curtains. But I was scared of the Red Room.

It was the room in which my uncle had died nine years before.

Bessie had told me that he was kind, and had brought me to live here after my parents died.

But his wife did not want me. His son, John, was a nasty bully, and his daughters were selfish and spiteful. Yet everyone loved them. The girls were pretty with their golden curls and silk dresses. I was plain and poor.

I wondered if my uncle's ghost was watching me now. I gripped my chair and stared into the gloom in panic. I did not want to see a ghost,

not even the ghost of my kind uncle.

A shadow moved across the ceiling.
I screamed and ran to the door.

'Let me out!' I banged the locked
door until my hands hurt. I was
angry and afraid.

But no one came. I curled up on
the floor and sobbed myself to sleep.

When I woke up, Bessie was standing over me. I was in a warm, comfortable bed. There was someone else in the room, too. It was Mr Lloyd, the apothecary. He was a kind man who gave us medicine when we were ill.

Bessie looked after me for the next few days. She made me a pastry tart but I wasn't hungry, and even when she offered to fetch me a book, I was too sad to read.

'How can you be sad?' said Mr

Lloyd when he called to see me again. 'You live in this lovely house with your aunt and cousins.'

'They hate me here, even though I try to be good,' I said. 'I wish I could run away.'

He seemed to believe me when I told him how unfairly I was treated.

'Would you like to go to school?' he asked.

I knew that if I went to school I would learn to paint and sew and play the piano. I would be allowed to read books, and learn French too. That sounded wonderful!

I looked up and gave him a small smile. 'Yes, I would like to go to school,' I said.

Mr Lloyd said he would speak to

my aunt. I waited for months, but
nothing happened. Meanwhile, my
cousins were not allowed to talk to
me, and I could not go to any of the
parties at Christmas.

One day, my aunt wanted to see
me. There was a man with her.
He had a serious face and bushy
eyebrows.

'Are you a good girl, Jane Eyre?'
he asked.

'No!' snorted my aunt. 'She's a
wicked child! I hope you will be

able to do something with her, Mr Brocklehurst.'

'I certainly will,' he said. 'We don't stand for any nonsense at Lowood School.'

I bit my lip to stop myself from crying out that I was not wicked. He wouldn't believe me, anyway.

Chapter Three

The next morning, I walked out of the front door with my small suitcase. It was still dark. I didn't look back at the house. I was very glad to leave.

I could see the lights and the horses' breaths as the coach neared.

My case was flung up onto the roof and the coachman opened the door and helped me inside. Then the door slammed shut and I left my aunt's house forever. I waved goodbye to Bessie. Leaving her was the only thing I was sad about.

It took all day to get to Lowood School and it was dark when I arrived.

I was taken to a room with a thick carpet, and paintings on the wall. A tall, dark-haired lady sat at

a desk. She had a gentle face and
smiled as I entered.

'You must be tired and hungry,
Jane,' she said.

I nodded, amazed at how kind her voice sounded. Maybe I could trust her.

She took me to a large room with about eighty girls sitting at two long tables. They all wore

brown wool dresses and white
pinafores. There was a drink of
water and a piece of oatcake for
each person.

Despite the kind lady, I felt quite
frightened.

After supper we said prayers. Then we were shown up to the bedrooms. There were several beds in each room. I fell asleep in mine immediately.

I shivered all night under the thin sheets, and in the morning we could not wash because the water in our bowls was frozen. After prayers we went to our classes. Later, I was given a cloak and bonnet to wear over the top of my clothes, and we all went outside onto a lawn. I stood by myself near the wall of the school.

Above the door something was carved into the stone.

LOWOOD
INSTITUTION
THIS HOUSE WAS BUILT IN 1813
BY NAOMI BROCKLEHURST, OF
BROCKLEHURST HALL

Then I saw a girl. She was sitting on a bench reading a book. As she turned the page she looked up and saw me watching her.

'What does *Lowood Institution* mean?' I asked, pointing at the words above the door.

'This is a charity school for orphans,' she said. 'Mrs Brocklehurst started the school. Now her son runs it.'

'Oh. So the tall, dark-haired lady isn't in charge, then?'

The girl laughed. 'Miss Temple? I wish she was. Mr Brocklehurst is the vicar. You'll meet him soon.'

My heart sank. I had already met him, and he didn't like me.

Chapter Four

My new friend was called Helen Burns. Even when she was in trouble for no reason, she took her punishment calmly. I knew that I would not be able to do this. Our teacher, Miss Scatcherd, was very unkind. She would always find

something to scold Helen about.
More than once I saw her hit
Helen on the neck with a bundle of
long twigs.

One day Mr Brocklehurst
came into the classroom. I was so
nervous at the sight of this
big, cruel-looking man, that
I dropped my writing
slate. It smashed
on the floor.

'Careless child!' he shouted.
Then he recognised me. 'Come
here, girl!'

I was frozen with fear. He
pointed to a stool and demanded I
stand on it.

He turned to all of the children
in my class. 'You see this girl?' he
asked. 'She is an evil girl with a
violent temper. Do not speak to her.
She is to stay there for half an hour.'

My cheeks burnt with anger
and shame. All my life I had been

accused of things I hadn't done.
Tears came to my eyes, but I was
determined not to cry in front of
everyone. Then Helen passed close
by me and smiled. That small act of
friendship gave me courage.

Later, when everyone had gone, I climbed down just as Helen came in with a tray of bread and milk.

'Helen, you are not supposed to speak to me. Everyone thinks I am bad.'

She shook her head. 'No, they don't. No one likes Mr Brocklehurst, and they won't believe him.'

Then, Helen started coughing badly. I put my arms around her.

We heard someone come through the door and turned in alarm. But it was only Miss Temple. 'I came to find you,' she said. 'Please come to my room, both of you.'

We sat in cosy armchairs by her fire.

'I shall judge you by your behaviour here, Jane, not by what I have heard. Now please tell me about yourself,' she said.

I told her about my aunt, my cruel cousins, and the Red Room. I told her how no one had ever liked me, but that I wanted to be calmer, like Helen, instead of angry. I didn't see how I could do that, now that the whole school thought I was wicked. I also mentioned Mr Lloyd, the apothecary, and Miss Temple said she knew him.

'I will write to him,' she said. 'If he agrees with your story, I can tell everyone that you are telling the truth.'

She went to a cupboard and took out a whole fruitcake with nuts on top. What heaven! No one except Bessie had ever been so kind to me.

Mr Lloyd must have replied to Miss Temple, because just a few weeks

later she told the whole school that the things that had been said about me were not true. Everyone clapped at the news.

It was foggy and wet all winter and we shivered in our beds every night. At last, spring arrived. I loved to walk in the valley surrounding Lowood, and to see the crocuses and primroses splashing colour in the dappled sunlight.

But being in the valley was not healthy. The dampness from winter

lingered. It crept into our lungs.
We never had enough to eat, so we
were weak. When a disease called
typhus came, many girls could not
fight it off and died.

I was lucky. I did not get sick,
so I was able to roam the hills and
woodland. I wished Helen could come
with me – but she could not. She
was ill too, though not with typhus.
The cough she had was serious. It
was a disease of the lungs called
tuberculosis, and there was no cure.

No one would tell me how she was doing, so one night I crept into her room.

'Helen,' I whispered. 'Are you awake?'

She opened her eyes. 'Is it you, Jane?'

She looked pale and thin, and began to cough.

I climbed into bed beside her and put my arms around her.

When I awoke in the morning, she was dead. She looked peaceful, and would not have to suffer that awful cough anymore. I cried, and knew I would miss her very much.

She was the first friend I had
ever had.

Mr Brocklehurst was blamed
for the illnesses in our school,
because he had not fed us properly,
or looked after us well enough.
Because of this, new people were
put in charge of the school and
things got much better.

Chapter Five

For the next six years I learnt many subjects including French and maths, and how to paint and play the piano.

After that, I stayed at the school for another two years as a teacher to the younger girls.

Miss Temple and I became very good friends. She had always been so kind to me and I owed her so much. But when she fell in love and left the school to get married, I knew it was time for me to move on. I was eighteen and desired to see more of the world.

I put an advert in the newspaper.

A young lady with teaching experience is looking for a job as a governess to children under fourteen. Able to teach French, drawing and music. Please reply to: JE, Post Office, Lowton, Yorkshire.

A week later there was a reply for me. I opened the envelope with excitement.

Mrs Fairfax,
Thornfield,
near Millcote, Yorkshire.

If JE can send a letter of reference of her abilities and character, there is a job with one pupil — a little girl — under ten years old. The salary is thirty pounds a year.

The next day I asked the school
governors for a letter of reference
and sent it to Mrs Fairfax.

This is to introduce Miss Jane Eyre.
She has been a pupil in this school for
six years and a teacher for two. She is
kind to her pupils and a good teacher.
She will make an excellent governess.

The positive letter got me the job,
and two weeks later I was on my

way to Thornfield Hall. I hoped that Mrs Fairfax would be a fair person, not like my aunt, Mrs Reed.

After travelling for sixteen hours, my coach stopped outside a large stone house. Candlelight glowed in one window, but otherwise it was dark. The horse stamped impatiently as the driver handed my luggage down from the roof.

My heart was thumping as I stood on the doorstep. I took a

deep breath and rang the bell. This
was the next chapter in my life.
Even though I was nervous,
I needed to see it as
an adventure.

A maid met me at the door and showed me into a snug room with a cosy fire. An elderly lady sat in an armchair. She was dressed in a black silk dress and white apron,

and wore a little cap on her head. She was knitting, and a large cat lay at her feet.

'How do you do, my dear?' she asked, smiling. 'You must be cold. Come closer to the fire.'

'Mrs Fairfax?' I asked.

She nodded and then spoke to the maid. 'Leah, please take Miss Eyre's luggage to her room and make her a hot drink and a sandwich.'

I was surprised to be treated like a visitor rather than a member of staff.

Mrs Fairfax explained that she was the housekeeper, and the owner of the house was called Mr Edward Rochester. He was away from home a lot. My pupil was a little French girl called Adèle, who was eight. Mr Rochester had adopted her when her mother stopped being able to look after her.

Chapter Six

When I awoke the next morning, my pretty bedroom was filled with sunshine. I got up and went for a walk outside and turned to look back at the house. It was built of grey stone with battlements around the roof, like a castle.

It was there that Mrs Fairfax
found me.

'How do you like Thornfield?'
she asked.

But I had no time to answer. A
little girl came running out of the

house. She
was a small,
pale child with
long curls
tumbling
down to her
waist.

'Good morning, Adèle,' said Mrs
Fairfax. 'Come and meet your new
governess, Miss Eyre.'

I spoke to her in French and
she was delighted. She said that I
spoke it as well as Mr Rochester.

That morning we had our
lessons. Afterwards, Mrs Fairfax
asked if I would like to see the view
from the roof. We stood on the
battlements and my heart warmed
at the sight of the rolling moors as
far as the eye could see.

'What kind of a man is Mr Rochester?' I asked her.

'He is a good man, but hard to read. It can be difficult to know when he is joking, and whether he is pleased or angry.'

I turned to go back downstairs. As I was going through the narrow, top floor corridor I heard a strange laugh. The sound made me shiver.

'Mrs Fairfax!' I called. 'Did you hear that laugh? Who is it?'

Mrs Fairfax came down and knocked on a door. 'Grace! Less noise!' She looked at me. 'It's just Grace Poole. She helps Leah and does some sewing.'

For a while I forgot about Grace Poole. I settled into my new routine, and was very happy at Thornfield. I had a lovely room to myself, and one pupil was not a lot of work, so I had time to go for long walks on the moors.

One cold day, I was walking back

from the village. The ground was hard and icy. I sat on a stile to rest for a moment. Then a big black-and-white dog came sniffing along the road.

I heard the clop-clop of a horse's hooves. As the horse and rider came into view, the horse slipped on a patch of ice and threw the rider onto the ground.

I ran to him. 'Are you hurt, sir? Can I fetch help?'

The man had a stern face with dark eyebrows.

He shook his head. 'You should be at home yourself. It is getting dark. Where do you live?'

'At Thornfield Hall, sir.'

'I see. Have you met Mr Rochester?'

'No, sir.'

'Please help me up.'

The man leant on my shoulder to

mount his horse. Then he galloped away with the dog at his heels.

When I arrived back at Thornfield Hall and walked into Mrs Fairfax's sitting room, I was surprised to see the same dog lying by the fire.

I rang the bell for Leah.

'Whose dog is this?' I asked. 'And where is Mrs Fairfax?'

'This is Pilot, Mr Rochester's dog. Mrs Fairfax is with the master now.'

So, I had already met my employer, Mr Edward Rochester. A serious man, not very friendly. Yet I did not fear him.

Chapter Seven

The next day, Adèle and I were asked to have tea with Mr Rochester. He had sprained his ankle in the fall, so he sat with his foot on a stool.

After tea, Adèle went away to play. Mr Rochester asked me to sit near him.

'How long have you been here?'
he asked.

'Three months, sir.'

'And where were you before?'

'I spent eight years at Lowood
School.'

He asked me a lot of questions about myself and asked me to play the piano. I did so, but after a moment he stopped me. 'I hope your other abilities are better than your playing,' he said.

I bristled at his rudeness but stopped myself from answering back. Then he scolded me for letting Adèle stay up so late, and I was dismissed. He seemed to be a stern man with little humour, but I suspected there was more to him.

One afternoon he met Adèle and I by chance in the garden. While Adèle played with Pilot, he told me a little about her mother, who was a dancer. He had loved her very much, but she had loved another man. As he spoke of her, his voice softened, and I could see the sadness on his face.

After this, we grew closer together. Sometimes I read to him and sometimes I just listened as he talked. We enjoyed one another's company. I could still see his faults.

He was often moody and could
be harsh. But, for some reason, I
could accept them.

I often heard Grace Poole's eerie
laughter from the room above, and
it always sent a shiver down my
spine. One night, after I had blown
out my candle and was just settling
down to sleep, I heard a scuffling
outside my door. I thought
that it was probably Pilot.

Then I heard that
strange laugh again.

It sounded very close. Was Grace Poole outside my room? I got up to see.

When I opened my door, I could smell smoke. I saw grey clouds drifting from under Mr Rochester's door. I rushed in. His four-poster bed was on fire.

'Mr Rochester!' I shouted. 'Wake up!'

I grabbed his water jug and flung the water over the flames. He leapt out of bed and beat out the fire.

74

'It's Grace Poole, sir. She tried to kill you.'

He took both of my hands in his. 'You saved my life, Jane. I knew you would do me good,' he said softly, looking into my face.

After this night, he often invited me to his study in the evening, and we discussed many subjects. He teased me for speaking plainly, especially when he asked if I thought him handsome, and I said he wasn't. He had a sharp wit, but so did I.

I began to look forward to seeing him and knew I was falling in love.

Then Blanche Ingram came to visit.

Chapter Eight

Miss Ingram was very beautiful: tall and graceful, with dark eyes and a proud look. It was rumoured that she and Mr Rochester would marry.

They were having a party one evening, which I was invited to join. I stood in the shadows in my dull

dress while the grand ladies wore silk

dresses and richly-coloured plumes.

I watched as Miss Ingram flirted

with Mr Rochester all evening, and

later she played the piano while

he sang. I needed to forget my love

for him. I was just a governess, and it was important for him to marry someone from a rich, important family.

This tore at my heart.

I left the party and went to bed.

The next day he went back with Miss Ingram and her family to stay at their house, and I tried to carry on my teaching of Adèle as usual.

'From there he may go abroad again,' said Mrs Fairfax. 'We may not see him again for a year.'

My heart sank. I felt very
miserable.

But Mr Rochester
did come back,
bringing along with
him many house
guests including
Miss Ingram. The
house was alive
and rang with
laughter.

I liked to walk
in the orchard

in the evening, especially with summer approaching. The air was warm and full of the scent of flowers.

One day, I turned a corner and there was Mr Rochester, bending over a bush.

'Come and look at this, Jane,' he said. 'It's a huge moth just like the ones in the West Indies.'

As I stood beside him I said, 'I will be very sad to leave, sir. I have grown to love it here, and will greatly miss Adèle and ... you.'

'Why must you go?'

'You have a bride.
I will not be
needed.'

'A bride,
where?' There
was a small
smile on his
face.

'Miss Ingram.'

'I am not
going to marry Miss
Ingram.'

He opened his arms. 'Come to me, Jane. Don't you know how I care for you?'

I went to him gladly and laid my head against his chest.

Edward Rochester raised my face to his and kissed my lips. 'Will you marry me, my darling?'

I looked into his eyes to see if he was teasing me, but he was not.

My heart nearly burst with happiness. 'Yes, sir. I will marry you.'

The wedding was to be a month later. Edward wanted me to wear his family jewels but I would not. I liked things plain and simple.

There was only ourselves, Mrs Fairfax and the minister at the church. He began the service.

'If anyone knows any reason why these two people should not marry, say it now.'

Suddenly there was a noise at the back of the church and a man ran in. 'They cannot marry!' he shouted. 'Mr Rochester has a wife already.'

I felt faint and Edward grabbed me to stop me from falling.

Chapter Nine

'A wife!' he said. 'Come with me and see my wife. I am married to a madwoman.'

He took my hand and we went back to the house. He took us up to the attic room where Grace Poole lived. When he opened the door, someone else was there too. The woman was wearing plain clothes and had long, unwashed hair. Her eyes were red from crying, but she laughed the same laugh I'd heard so often. Grace Poole sat by the fire, sewing.

'This is my wife,' said Edward.
'My parents forced me to marry her
when I was younger. She was a nice
person for a while, until the madness
came. She is well looked after here
by Grace Poole. I would never send
her to a cruel asylum.'

At that moment, the poor woman
sprang up and lunged towards
Edward.

The man who had burst into the
church was the woman's brother,
Mr Mason. He and the vicar

grabbed her, and at last Grace Poole managed to tie her hands together.

It was such a pitiful sight.

We went downstairs again and Edward and I were alone.

'We must go away, Jane,' he said. 'I have another house where we can live together.'

But I knew the shame of living together without being married. I knew that people would whisper behind my back. They would shun me in the street and refuse to serve me in the shops. I would be an outcast. But most of all I would not be happy, because it was against what I believed in. I needed to keep to my principles, even if it meant never seeing Edward again.

It took all the strength I had, but I said goodbye to Edward Rochester and walked out of the house into the night. He had begged me on his knees to stay, and we both cried. But if I stayed, I would regret it. It was the hardest thing I had ever done.

I had thirty shillings and asked the coachman to take me as far as my money would pay.

After many hours, he dropped me in a small village. I had no money and few belongings so I knocked on doors to beg for food and shelter, but most were shut in my face.

At last a vicar found me lying on his doorstep. I was soaking wet and cold. I would have died if he and his sisters had not taken me in and looked after me.

When I was well, the vicar told me his name was St John Rivers. He was a tall, slim man with a finely-shaped face, pale eyes and blond hair. St John's sisters were called Diana and Mary. I told them my name was Jane Elliot. I didn't want anyone to know my real name in case Edward Rochester came looking for me.

They were surprised that I had been to school for six years. They thought that I was a beggar.

'We are both governesses too,'

said Diana, 'but our mother recently died so we came to stay with St John for the funeral.'

When St John found out I was a teacher, he said that I could work at the new school that was opening. I was delighted at the idea.

The ladies and I became great friends during the next few weeks. I liked them very much. But I did not like St John. His manner was cold and unfriendly, and he never showed any emotion.

The school opened and I became a teacher to the village children. In my spare time I enjoyed painting and drawing. One day St John was looking at a picture I had painted, and he pointed to my signature.

Eyre

'I thought so,' he said. 'Elliott is not your real name. I have asked around. You are Miss Jane Eyre of Thornfield Hall. Before that you lived with your aunt, Mrs Reed.'

I nodded.

'We are cousins, Jane,' he said. 'Our uncle, John Eyre, has recently died in Madeira. He has left you all his money.'

I was astonished. This uncle had written to me at my aunt's house. Because I no longer lived there,

I never received the letter.

St John showed me his letter from his solicitor.

Mr St John Rivers,
Moor House,
Marsh End, Yorks.

Dear Sir,

Your uncle, Mr John Eyre, has died at his home in Madeira. He has left all his money — a sum of £20,000 — to his niece, Miss Jane Eyre. We understand that you know of her whereabouts.

I was now a very rich woman, but I didn't think it fair that I should have all of the money. We were all equally related to John Eyre. So, I divided the money equally as well. St John, Diana, Mary and I each got five thousand pounds.

Chapter Ten

Over the next year, I enjoyed teaching at the school. Then, St John asked me to marry him and go with him to India, where he was going to be a missionary. India sounded like such an exciting place, and I longed to see more of the world. But I knew that St John wanted someone to help with his work rather than be a wife. Added to that, I did not love him, and it was so very far away from Thornfield and Edward Rochester. I said no.

I wondered what had become of him. I had written to Mrs Fairfax a month before but had no answer.

St John was not so easily put off by my refusal. He asked me to marry him many times.

One day he came close to me and rested a hand on my head. 'You *will* be my wife,' he said.

Maybe I had been wrong to say no. What else would I do with my life? I was slowly giving in. Suddenly, I heard a voice in my head as clearly as if it were real.

'Jane! Jane! Jane!'

It was Edward Rochester. A strong feeling washed over me. He needed me.

'I am coming!' I shouted.

The next day I packed up my things and left on a coach. It dropped me at an inn close to Thornfield Hall.

I almost ran the last mile. I longed to be there. To see him. I was almost there …

Then I stopped in shock.

Thornfield Hall was a ruin. A great fire had burnt the place and its black jagged stonework clawed at the sky.

I sank to the ground and sobbed.

Later, at the inn, I was told that the fire had been started by Mr Rochester's mad wife. He had gone into the blazing building to try to save her. She had died and he had been severely burnt. He had lost a hand and was blind.

Now he lived at his other house. I asked the landlord to take me there immediately.

Ferndean Manor was not a grand building like Thornfield Hall. It was much smaller and was buried deep in a wood.

Edward was sitting in his chair by the fireside, with Pilot at his feet. The dog looked up and wagged his tail.

'Is that you, Mary?' He turned, expecting the maid.

'Well, Pilot knows who I am,' I said.

I watched the expression on his face. He reached out and grabbed my hand. 'It is *her* hand,' he said, his voice breaking with emotion. 'It is *her* fingers, *her* voice. Am I

dreaming, or has my Jane come
back to me?'

   'I have come back to you,
Edward.'

   My eyes filled with tears. I knelt
in front of him and hugged this
wonderful man that I
loved so much.

I pressed my lips to his.

'I called for you, Jane, and you came,' he said, stroking my hair.

He asked me where I had been all that time. I told him everything that had happened and that I was a rich woman.

'But how can you love me? I'm blind and have only one hand. You are an independent woman now.'

'And I love you more than ever,' I said.

Reader, I married him.

During the next year, Edward's health improved. I became his eyes. I read to him and guided him about the house.

In time, he gained a little sight in one eye. I fell pregnant, and when our son was born, my heart was filled with joy. Edward could see him.

My fingers closed round a small, ice-cold hand. With horror, I tried to pull my hand back but the fingers tightened. An eerie voice said, 'Let me in!'

Many years ago, a young homeless boy was taken in at Wuthering Heights. Older now, Heathcliff is set on revenge and destroying everybody around him. And there is a lonely ghost roaming the moors, who is determined to be reunited with her lover ...